Children's Adoration Prayer Book

Bob Hartley & Deeper Waters Team
Illustrations by Mercy Clonts

ISBN 978-0-615-58840-7

Printed in the United States

ACKNOWLEDGMENTS

Jeremy Butrous- Thank you for spearheading this project and helping it come to fruition. What a blessing you are to the team, you are highly valued and appreciated!

Janna Butrous- Thank you for your time spent as you invested into this book. Your heart for Adoration and Children will surely bless the World!

Nicole Gay- Thank you for your envisioning of an Adoration book for children. Your matriarchal heart has touched so many. We are so grateful for you, Nicole!

Leela Kim- We are so thankful for your time spent at Deeper Waters, Leela. You have been a blessing in so many ways. Thank you for helping with this project and so many others, we will forever be grateful for your time with us!

Mercy Clonts- Wow! What a beautiful work you have done for this book. Your illustrations and pictures have touched Deeper Waters and will touch children from all over the World. Thank you immensely for your teamwork on this book!

PARENT'S PAGE

Hello Parents! What an awesome experience you have available to partner with the God who created your little ones! He has chosen you in raising your Children to bless the Lord and love Him well all the days of their lives. We honor and value your role as a parent as you impart, teach and nurture your children. This book is designed to assist you, as you point your precious ones to the Father.

Psalm 78 talks about not hiding, but showing the generation to come; the praises of the Lord and declaring His goodness to them that they may set their HOPE in God.

"We will not hide them from their children, showing to the generations to come, the praises of the Lord, and his strength, and his wonderful works that he hath done. For he established a testimony in Jacob and appointed a law in Israel, which he commanded our fathers, that they should make them known to their children: That the generation to come might know them, even the children which should be born; who should arise and declare them to their children: That they might set their hope in God, and not forget the works of God but keep his commandments."

- Psalm 78:4-8

We bless you as parents, guardians, and loved ones to sow seeds of Hope and the Knowledge of God in this next generation now, that they may be the reformers of tomorrow!

What is ADORATION PRAYER?

Adoration, or "Face to Face" prayer, is loving and magnifying the Lord above all else and in every circumstance and season of life. It is setting our eyes on the prize, of knowing Christ Jesus and delighting in who He is. A person in love can do anything! Adoration brings us into a state of falling in love with Him and giving Him the love He is due! To adore Him is to look into His eyes. It is not just talking about Him, or around Him, but TO Him. When we adore the Lord, we behold Him in all His glory!

Adoration is giving our entire devotion. It is not about making requests of Him, but offering Him our whole heart and all of our affection. It is a moment of thanking Him for who He is and declaring His nature in and over every area of our life.

When we begin to adore Him - that is when we encounter Him! He hears our invitation, comes near to us, and blesses us with His presence as He dwells among us. What a beautiful way to encounter our Lord!

-Scriptures Referencing Adoration And Magnifying The Lord-

1. Psalm 8:2 "From the lips of children and infants you have ordained praise because of your enemies, to silence the foe and the avenger."

A. It was in the Lord's heart that children should adore Him and make His name great in all the Earth. He delights in the sound of their voices and it is their destiny to bring glory to His name. It is such an honor that children get to move the heart of God through adoration. As His heart is loved, our enemies are silenced – how awesome is the power of adoration!

2. Psalm 22:3 "Yet you are holy, O You who are enthroned upon the praises of Israel."

A. The Lord sits enthroned on our praises! As we come into agreement with His Kingship, we release his power and authority in the earth realm! He has given authority of the Earth to the sons of man, and we have the great privilege to usher in His dominion through our worship and agreement with Him.

B. Adoration is the pattern we see in heaven! The Lord is surrounded by worship and adoration continually throughout all of eternity. When we come into agreement with heaven, we release that glory and majesty into our surroundings on Earth… "on Earth as it is in Heaven!"

Personal Example of Adoration: Story of My Dad at Christmas

-Bob Hartley-

When I was a child, the kids in my family would give my father goofy gifts for Christmas. We would take turns presenting silly poems or witty jokes to him. My siblings were all very bright and could be quite entertaining. My dad always played along with this tradition in good fun.

One year, however, the routine changed. My oldest sister began to read her poem, but for some reason she couldn't continue. She crumpled the paper she held in her hand, threw it to the floor and looked my dad in the eyes. "Dad, I have never met a man like you. You are as gentle a man I have ever known. You are so honorable and kind."

My brother picked up where she left off, "Yeah Dad. You never get worried and burdened you always turn hard things into joyful things." Another sister shared, "When I get married, Dad I want to marry a man like you." The next brother began, "Dad, you are unpretentious, you never pretend. You are so sincere and I want to grow up to be a man like you."

I tucked myself behind the Christmas tree and cried. I loved to see my father loved, hoped in, believed in, and appreciated, as he had done for us countless times! It so moved my heart to see my father's heart cared for and valued in that way.

That Christmas, I learned firsthand about the power of adoration. I saw how this love and affection made my father feel valued and loved and how my heart came alive as his heart was cared for in an appropriate way. I realized that our Father in Heaven desires our love and affection as His sons and daughters. My heart was so touched and moved to see him adored this way.

Suggested Use Of This Book

This book was written to help your children begin their own personal journey to encounter the God of Hope. This Adoration Book can be used along side any regular bible reading, family devotional times, or even times of artistic expression by your children. After continuous use, they learn to adore the Lord in the morning, afternoon, and even at bedtime. Feel free to allow them to have fun discovering how loving God is and how much He cares for them!

There are four main components to each letter: Faces of God, a Supporting Scripture, Adoration Sentence, and "Let's Pray Together".

Faces of God – These are attributes or descriptions of who God is from A to Z. There are two faces per letter that were derived from the original Adoration Prayer Book created by Bob Hartley/Deeper Waters Ministry. There are thousands more faces of God, many undiscovered. Perhaps this book will encourage your children to explore the different faces of God and even search for the ones yet to be known.

Supporting Scripture - There are more scriptures that support each face. We listed one scripture per face. However this is a perfect opportunity for you and your children to go on a treasure hunt in the Word to find more scriptures that reveal that particular face.

Adoration Sentence – This area was designed to launch your children in the discovery of each face of God. The intent is to introduce or reinforce the knowledge of God. Feel free to dialogue with your children about truths pertaining to that particular face of God. It is our hope and prayer that your children will love to learn about and adore the God who desires to be known!

Let's Pray Together –During this time, after the particular face has been introduced and discussed, you and your child can join together and ask the Lord for more and then declare His attributes over your life. He desires to encounter both you and your children, so be encouraged to go before Him as a family to allow Him to hear your heart and bless you together!

Aa

You are the God I can always **APPROACH**.

Scripture:
"Jesus said, 'Let the little children come to me, and do not hinder them, for the Kingdom of Heaven belongs to such as these." – Matthew 19:14

Adoration Sentence:
Papa God, You are so easy to talk to. You are so approachable; I know I can spend my moments with You at anytime. I am so glad that You are the God that always let's me run to You, and be with You. Your arms are always open wide for me! You have made me feel at home in Your arms.

Let's Pray Together:
God, I thank You that You are approachable. Thank You that You love to give us hugs and kisses. And You love when I give my family hugs and kisses too. Help us as a family to remember that we can always approach You, and be near to You. You are a faithful God and You will never turn us away. We love spending moments with You!
In Jesus name – Amen

You are the God who always **ACCEPTS** me.

Scripture:
"Accept one another, just as Christ accepted you, in order to bring praise to God." – Romans 15:7

Adoration Sentence:
You accept me for who I am. You receive me – it's TRUE!! You welcome me into Your loving embrace, into all of who You are. Through Your Son Jesus, You've accepted me into Your family and now I am Your child, a child of God. Your Word says that You have prepared a place for me. That's AMAZING. You are so accepting, I am even welcomed into Your home. Thank you Jesus

Let's Pray Together:
Father, I thank You for accepting me just the way I am. You are such a good Father to your children! You not only love me, but You like me too. You even like the things I like, because You put them in my heart. Help me to remember that You always accept me no matter what I say or do. Teach my heart to know, that I have no need to fear in life, because Your accepting love keeps me safe. In Jesus name Amen.

Bb

You are the **BEAUTIFUL** God.

Scripture:
"One thing I ask of the Lord. This is what I seek – that I may dwell in the house of the Lord all the days of my life, to gaze upon the beauty of the Lord" – Psalm 27:4

Adoration Sentence:
Every day I wake up and I get to see all the wonderful things You've created! There are so many beautiful things to see; like animals, trees and my friends and families. They are all reflections of who You are. God, even the things that I think are the most beautiful- You are more beautiful than all of them. Your beauty is amazing; no one is more beautiful than You!

Let's Pray Together:
O God, who You are, and all that You have created is beautiful! Help me to have a heart like David and desire to look at Your beauty all the days of my life. When I look at Your beautiful face, somehow I realize just how beautiful You've made me too. It's fun to know that I am truly made in Your image. I pray that I will always look to You to show me, what true beauty is. In Jesus name – Amen!

You are the God who **BLESSES** me.

Scripture:
"The same Lord is Lord of all and richly blesses all who call on Him". – Romans 10:12

Adoration Sentence:
You are a Good Father who loves to bless Your children with everything they need. You sent the greatest blessing to Earth when You sent Your Son, Jesus. Your word says, "Every good and perfect gift comes from You" and You never run out of gifts to bless Your children with. I look to You with open hands and an open heart ready to receive all the blessings You have for me.

Let's Pray Together:
Thank You Lord for all the blessings You have given me! Thank You so much for my family. I want to pray a blessing over them. May You bless them with Your love, while they are at home and at work! May You bless their dreams, hopes and desires! Jesus, would You help me be a blessing to my family and to the world? I want to bless others that same way You have blessed me! I want to bless You all the days of my life!
In Jesus name- Amen.

Cc

You are the God who **CARES** about me.

Scripture:
"Cast all your cares upon Him, for He cares for you."– 1 Peter 5:7

Adoration Sentence:
You are such a caring God. You even cared for all the animals when You put them on Noah's Ark to be safe. You care about me, and how I feel and even about all the things I do. You care about my school, my teachers, my friends and You really care about my future! Wow God, You really do care for me! And You know what? I really care for You too!

Let's Pray Together:
Jesus, I know You will always care for me. Like the scripture says, I don't have to worry because You care about me. You not only care for me, but You also care for ALL Your sons and daughters. Jesus, will You teach me how to care for others the same way You care for me? Thank You for being a caring God. In Jesus name- Amen.

You are the God who is **CLOSE** to me.

Scripture:
"Come close to God and He will come close to you" – James 4:8 (Amp).

Adoration Sentence:
I see Your face as the close God, the near one, who never leaves me and will never forsake me. You are with me when I go to bed at night and You are with me when I wake up in the morning. You are even with me when I eat my breakfast! You are right here with me at ALL times. I am never alone because You are always close to me!

Let's Pray Together:
Father thank You, that I can feel Your nearness through the Holy Spirit. Thank You that You carry me through my whole life. Every time I say the name Jesus, I can feel You and I know You're not far away. You are the God who wants to be close to me and I want to be close to You! In Jesus name – Amen!

Dd

You are the God who **DEFENDS** me.

Scripture:
"To You, O my Strength, I will sing praises; For God is my defense, My God of mercy."– Psalm 59:17

Adoration Sentence:
Jesus, You are my hero! You come to my rescue when I need help and You defend me. You shield me and cover me. Just like King David and how You gave him the confidence to never be afraid. You are the strongest defender I know and You will always protect me.

Let's Pray Together:
King Jesus, my awesome defender – I love you. I lift my hands towards You in praise, because You are my defense. Thank You for surrounding me with Your defending arms. I will always remember that You are the God who defends His children. In Jesus name – Amen.

You are the **DELIGHTFUL** God who delights in me.

Scripture:
"For the Lord takes delight in His people; He crowns the humble with Salvation." – Psalm 149:4

Adoration Sentence:
You are a Happy Delightful God. You enjoy me and take delight in me. Your delightful ways make life fun! You always know how to make me laugh and smile. Thank You that You dance over me with Your happy heart. Your song of delight and Your presence brings me joy. I will take delight in You forever.

Let's Pray Together:
Father, Your delight always makes me feel special and loved. Spending time with You everyday makes me feel delighted. Let me hear Your voice that rejoices in me when I am at home with my family or playing with my friends. I'm so grateful that You take delight in who I am! In Jesus name – Amen!

Ee

You are the **EVERLASTING FATHER.**

Scripture:
"For to us a child is born, to us a son is given, and the government will be on His shoulders. And He will be called Wonderful Counselor, Mighty God, Everlasting Father, Prince of Peace." - Isaiah 9:6

Adoration Sentence:
You are my Father, and You will always be my Father. I love that You are happy to be my Ever-Lasting Father, watching over me, protecting me, and providing for me. You last forever. Even toys sometimes break or fade away, but You never fade away. I can count on You to always be around. I love being Your child!

Let's Pray Together:
God I thank You for being the same yesterday, today and forever. I am so happy that I can count on You because You never change, You stay the same. You were alive before the Earth was made and You will be until the end of time. Thank You that Your love for me and my family is never ending. Teach me how to have a never ending love, like You my Everlasting Father. In Jesus name- Amen.

You are the **EVER-PRESENT** God.

Scripture:
"God is our refuge and strength, an ever present help in trouble". - Psalm 46:1

Adoration Sentence:
Holy Spirit, You are always with me. You walk beside me and You are ever-present in my life. Your presence is so important to me and Your nearness reminds me of the promises that are in Your heart. I love that You chose to stay right by my side even before I asked You to. Thank You for always being near. I love You, my Ever-Present God!

Let's Pray Together:
Heavenly Father, You are the one we draw near to. Instruct us in Your wisdom the same way You instructed King Solomon. You never left him, and I know You will never leave me. My Ever-Present God, You are my Good Shepherd. Teach me how I can stay connected to You at all times. Without You, my life is not fun, but with You my life is full of happiness! In Jesus name – Amen.

Ff

You are the God who **FORGIVES** me.

Scripture:
"You are forgiving and good O Lord; abounding in love to all who call to You." – Psalm 86:5

Adoration Sentence:
God, You love us so much that You created a way for us to be forgiven, so that we can be close to You. You are filled with grace for those who need forgiveness, how amazing You are! You choose love instead of punishment. And You freely give us Your mercies because You have love and forgiveness in Your heart.

Let's Pray Together:
Heavenly Father, can You teach me more about forgiveness? Help me to show others forgiveness, the way You do. I want to be like You and Your loving ways. I know everyone deserves mercy and I want to show others Your mercy too. Thank You, for always being willing to forgive, so that we may be close to You! In Jesus name -Amen.

You are the God of **FRIENDSHIP.**

Scripture
"No longer do I call you servants... But I have called you friends."
- John 15:15

Adoration Sentence:
Jesus, what a good friend You are! You are my favorite friend. I know You are a good friend because You spent time with Adam and walked in the garden with him. Even though You have more friends that I can count, You still have time for me! Thank You for being my best friend.

Let's Pray Together:
Jesus, I can't believe it, I am a friend of God! Teach me how to be an amazing friend to others, just like You are to me. I want to be as kind and loving as You are. Thank You for being the God of Friendship. I'm so happy that my friends at school and church are friends with You too. Our friendship really blesses me. In Jesus name- Amen.

Gg

You are the **GOOD SHEPHERD**.

Scripture:
I am the Good Shepherd; I know my sheep and my sheep know me."
- John 10:14

Adoration Sentence:
I am Your sheep and You are my Shepherd. As my Shepherd You love to feed me, lead me and watch over me. It is Your heart's desire for me to know Your voice, follow Your heart, and stay in the safety of Your watch. I don't have to be afraid of where I go because You guide me. You know just what I need and You have blessed my paths. I trust You as my Good Shepherd.

Let's Pray Together:
Lord, You were a Good Shepherd to King David. You led him beside still waters and refreshed His soul. I know You will do the same for me and guide me along the right paths. With You as my Good Shepherd, I lack nothing. Help me to know Your voice and know Your heart. Thank You that You hold my hand as I follow You, and You never let me go. You truly are my Good Shepherd. In Jesus name- Amen.

You are the **GLAD GOD** who makes us glad by all you do.

Scripture:
This is the day the Lord has made; let us rejoice and be glad in it.
-Psalm 118:24

Adoration Sentence:
You are such a happy and glad God! You smile and You dance over me because You love me. God, You are so happy about who You created me to be. I love living life knowing that You smile and rejoice over me. Every day You have made, I will be glad in it.

Let's Pray Together:
God, You are the most glad-hearted one I know. Help me to know more of how glad You are and how glad I make You. Show me Your happy heart and how I can carry Your joy and show it to my family and friends.
In Jesus name – Amen

Hh

You are the God who **HELPS** me.

Scripture:
"Behold, God is my helper; The Lord is with those who uphold my life"
– Psalm 54:4

Adoration Sentence:
The same God that created the Heaven's and the Earth, bends down to help me when I am in need. Holy Spirit, You help me anytime I need You. You love helping me with learning and my homework! You even help me when I'm helping my parents around the house. Thank You for being my helper.

Let's Pray Together:
Father, Your word says that I can find all of the help I need in You. You always hear my voice and like to help! Please teach me to trust You and look to You for help when I am at home, or school, or even with friends. I need Your help more than I realize sometimes. Send Your Helper, the Holy Spirit, to stay with me and be my helper through my whole life. In Jesus name – Amen!

You are the God who **HEALS.**

Scripture:
"... I am the Lord Who heals you." – Exodus 15:26

Adoration Sentence:
Lord, You are a healer to all. You mend broken hearts and You touch hurting bodies. I know if I fall down and scrape my knee, You can take away my pain. All I have to do is say "In Jesus name, be healed". Jesus, You healed everyone You prayed for in the Bible. Your Presence heals those who are lonely and Your happy heart heals those who are sad. You have blessed the world with Your healing touch and loving heart!

Let's Pray Together:
Thank You Heavenly Father for being such a great God that heals. Nothing is impossible for You. Holy Spirit, come and teach me more about Jesus, the healer. Show me how I can be one who prays for healing the same way Jesus did. I am not afraid to pray for those who are sick because You said the same power that raised Christ from the dead, lives in me! I desire to do the works that Jesus did. Thank You for giving me faith and power through Your Word to do so! In Jesus name- Amen.

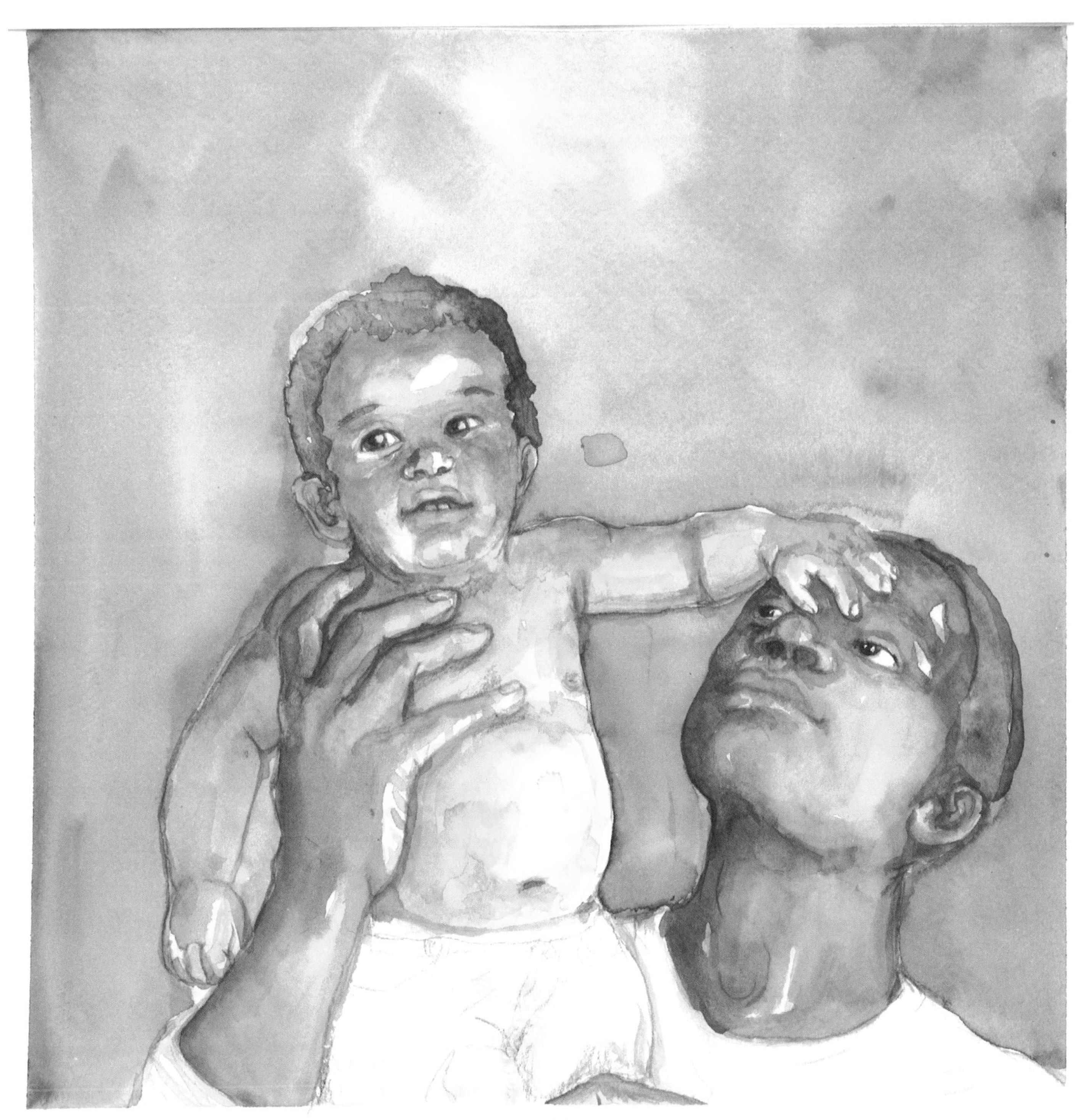

You are the God who **INSTRUCTS** me.

Scripture:
"He will instruct you and teach you in the way you should go."
– Psalms 32:8

Adoration Sentence:
God, You have instructed people since the beginning of time. When I read Your Word, I see how You taught Abraham, Moses, David, and so many others. You taught them how to build, how to worship and how to be a friend to You. When they didn't know what to do or where to go, You instructed them, just like my parents at home instruct me. You are the wisest and best instructor I know.

Let's Pray Together:
God, You love to teach me and I want to learn from You. Will You teach me how to love You and learn from Your understanding? Thank You that You send the Holy Spirit to help me make the right decisions. Help me also to listen to my parents instructions because I know they listen to You.
In Jesus name- Amen.

You are the God of the **IMPOSSIBLE.**

Scripture:
"For nothing is impossible with God" – Luke 1:37

Adoration Sentence:
When I think about all the miracles You did in the Bible, I see that nothing impossible with You! I know I can do all things with You because You can do the impossible. You can rescue me from anything! I want a life filled with Your miracles.

Let's Pray Together:
God, I will always believe that You are the God of miracles, signs, wonders and impossibilities. I ask for faith to trust You with every situation I'm in. Thank You for the miracles You have for me and my family. Help me to always believe in Your astounding ways. In Jesus name – Amen.

Jj

You are **JESUS CHRIST.**

Scripture:
"For God so loved the World, that He gave His one and only begotten Son. That whoever believes in Him, will not perish or die but have everlasting life."- John 3:16

Adoration Sentence:
Jesus Christ, You are my greatest treasure. You gave your life for me so I could know You forever. Thank You that You love me so much, and You desire me.   Here is my heart - I give it to You, like You gave me Yours – Jesus I love You!

Let's Pray Together:
Jesus, Thank You that Your love for me outstretches the sky and outnumbers the sand on the beach. I want to know all about how You feel for me and the plans You have for me. Help me to live a life that makes You smile and brings You great joy. Help me to love You and follow You. Help my family and friends, that they would know how You feel about them too. In Jesus name – Amen!

You are the **GOD OF JOY**

Scripture:
"The Lord your God is in the midst of you, a Mighty One, a Savior! He will rejoice over you with joy." Zephaniah 3:17

Adoration Sentence:
You are the God of joy and laughter. Thank You that You took joy in creating me to be me! My happiness doesn't come from what toys I have and how many people like me, but it comes from You. You are the most happy and joyful one I know. You are the reason for my happiness; You are the reason for my joy.

Let's Pray Together:
God of Joy, come and fill me with Your Spirit. Give me the joy that is in Your heart that keeps me belly laughing with You. Fill my mouth with much laughter and help me to bring laughter and joy to others around me. In Jesus name – Amen.

Kk

You are the **KIND GOD.**

Scripture:
"I have loved you with an everlasting love; I have drawn you with Loving-kindness." - Jeremiah 31:3

Adoration Sentence:
You are kindest and most compassionate person I know. You show me Your kindness in every area of my life. Thank You for the way You take care for me. What would I do without Your kindness? You show me how others should be treated with kindness too.

Let's Pray Together:
Jesus, reveal how kind You are to me today. Can You show Your kindness to me when I play sports, activities and games? I know that sometimes, I should be more kind to others no matter if I win or lose, but You are ALWAYS kind no matter what. I invite You into my life today my Kind God! In Jesus name - Amen.

You are the **KING OF KINGS.**

Scripture:
"God, the blessed and only Ruler, the King of Kings and Lord of Lords." – 1 Timothy 6:15

Adoration Sentence:
Since the beginning, there have been Kings and Queens on the Earth. Some good, some bad, some strong, some weak, and many thought they were the best that ever lived. But when I think about You Jesus – King of all Kings, no one can compare to You! At Your name, every knee will bow and every tongue will confess that You are King, You are Lord. You are awesome, and I desire to serve You forever!

Let's Pray Together:
Jesus – Ruler, King, and Lord You are so wise and so strong. I want to know more about You as my King. Teach me how to serve You, King Jesus, because You are worthy of my life. No one can compare to You. I thank You for Your leadership in my life yesterday, today and forever.
In Jesus name – Amen.

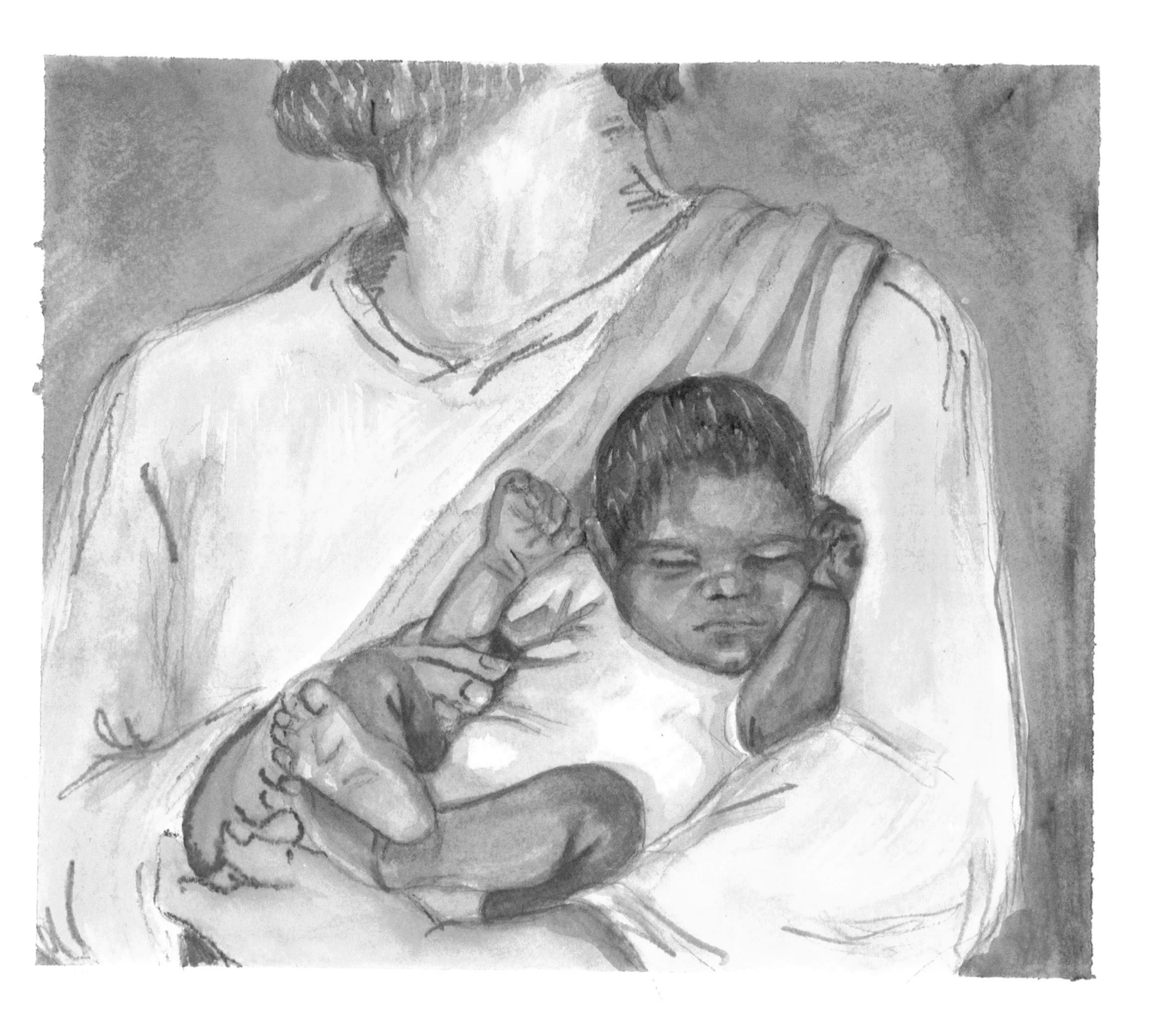

You are **THE LISTENING GOD.**

Scripture:
"With my voice I cry to the Lord, and He hears and answers me out of His holy hill." Psalm 3:4

Adoration Sentence:
Your listening heart is beautiful. You are a talking God and You are a Listening God too! You listen to what my mouth says and You also listen to what my heart says. You say to me in Your word that You love to hear my voice and that my voice is sweet and my face is lovely. It's amazing to know that the God who stretched out the Heavens like a curtain is the same God who bends down to hear my voice when I call. Thank You for always listening to me.

Let's Pray Together:
Father, thank You for Your desire to listen to me. It makes me feel so very special to know that my voice is important to You. You love to listen to me, and I love listening to what You have to say to me. I know You desire to tell me Your secrets. Show me what questions I can ask of You that will bring me closer to You. I know I can always talk to You!
In Jesus name – Amen!

You are the **LOVING GOD.**

Scripture:
"For as high as the Heavens are above the Earth, so great is His love..."
Psalm 103:11

Adoration Sentence:
There will never be anyone in the world that can love me like You do! You are the true meaning of love. Your love is so strong, so faithful, and never ends! You love me at all times, even when I'm sleeping! Your heart is so big that You have enough love for all the people on the Earth. That is ALOT of love. You truly are my Loving God!

Let's Pray Together:
Loving God, thank You for Your love that is so patient and kind, never failing and always forgiving. You had a love for me in Your heart before I was even born! Father, I know that You love me, not because of what I do, but because of who I am. I am Your child. Show me how to love others the way You have loved me, with a love that always believes the best in people. Your love is my hope that won't ever disappoint! In Jesus name – Amen!

Mm

You are the **MIGHTY GOD.**

Scripture:
"Who is this King of Glory, the Lord strong and mighty, the Lord mighty in battle." – Psalm 24:8

Adoration Sentence:
Jesus, You are my superhero! There is no one stronger or mightier than You. I am amazed at Your strength. I think about how You raised Jesus from the dead. How much power did it take for You to do that? If Your might was able to give Jesus life again, how much more will Your might heal those who are sick and save those who are lost? The Bible says Your hand is not so short that it cannot save. I believe Your power and might is strong enough to destroy any sickness. I look to You Mighty God, for You are mighty to save!

Let's Pray Together:
Heavenly Father, You are so mighty! You have more than enough might that I can look to You for strength. You save us from harm and lift us up to be seated next to You. Holy Spirit, can You show me how I can grow up to be a mighty child of God? I want to be mighty and help save others from harm and help lift them up too. Help me to grow strong in the Spirit so that I can be powerful just like my strong and mighty God!
In Jesus Name- Amen.

You are the **MERCIFUL GOD.**

Scripture:
"For the LORD is good; His Mercy is everlasting." – Psalm 100:5

Adoration Sentence:
Oh Lord, my God, You are the most merciful person I have ever known. You always choose to believe the best in people. You even give others second chances if they make mistakes. You never stop believing in Your people because You have so much mercy to show and give. Your Word says, surely Your mercy and goodness will follow me all the days of my life. Thank You that You have an unending supply of mercy and grace for me and for all Your children.

Let's Pray Together:
King Jesus, You have shown me kindness and mercy. I want to show You and my parents obedience and sometimes I need extra mercy to do that. Thank You that You delight in showing me mercy so that I will grow up and be the best person I can be. I want to also show others mercy, so that they too will show other people Your mercy. Lord, I desire to be like King David and sing of Your mercies forever! In Jesus name – Amen.

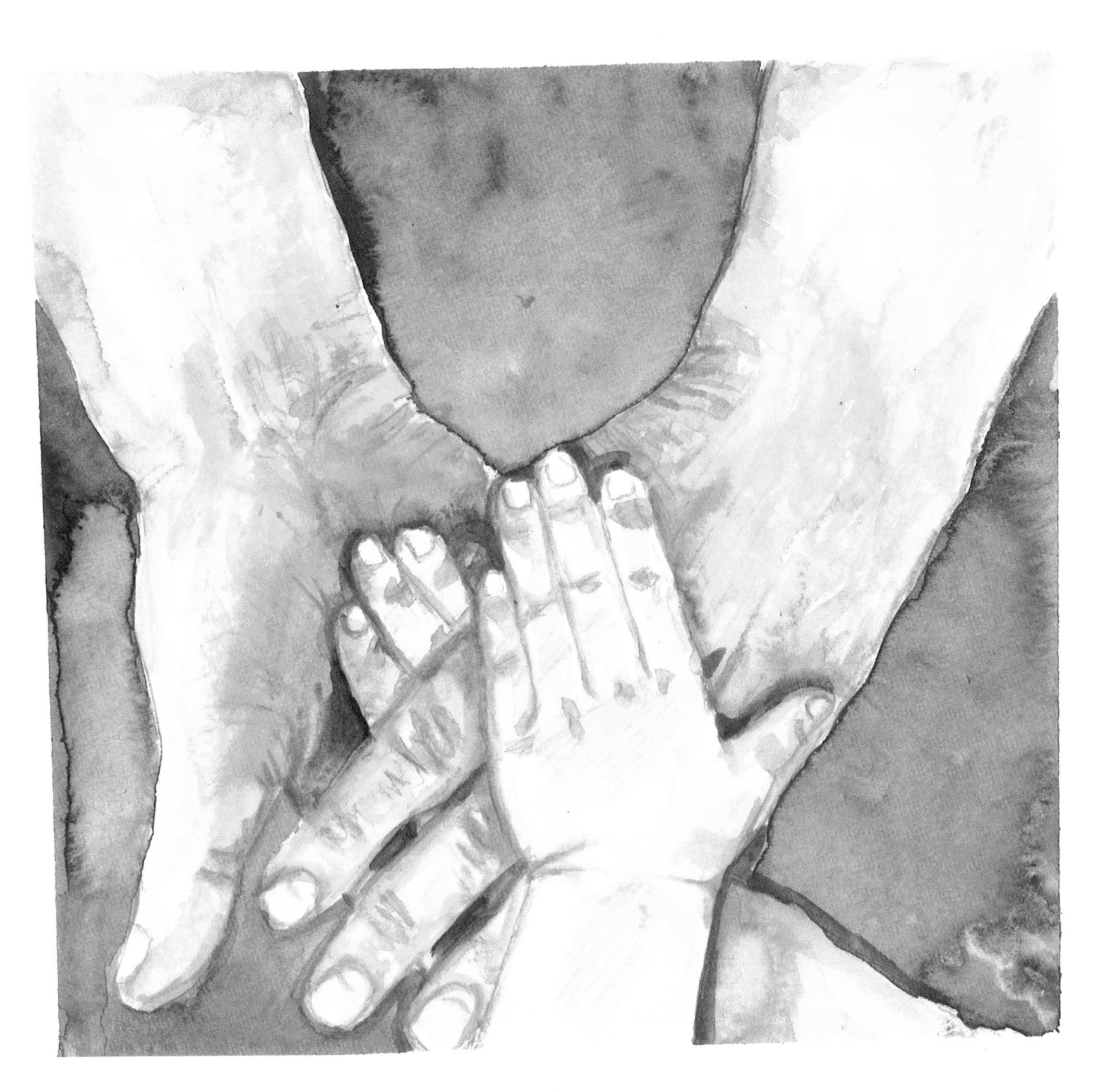

Nn

You are the **NAME ABOVE ALL NAMES GOD.**

Scripture:
"Therefore God exalted him to the highest place and gave him the Name that is above every Name." – Philippians 2:9

Adoration Sentence:
There is no name like the name of JESUS. You have the most famous name ever! Things happen when I speak Your name because Your name has power and life. Your name causes the lame to walk and the blind to see. It is because of Your name that I can go to the Father and spend time with Him. It is Your name that every knee will bow to, that is in Heaven and those on the Earth. That means everything created will acknowledge You as Lord. What a name!

Let's Pray Together:
Jesus, I am blown away by the power that is in Your name. Your name is the name that is above every other name and I get to declare it every day! How holy is Your wonderful and beautiful name, Jesus. When I speak Your name, I know I can bring change into the World. I can't wait to see what good things will happen in my life when I speak and depend on Your name. May Your name be upon my lips, all the days of my life.
In Jesus name – Amen.

You are the **NEVER FAILING GOD.**

Scripture:
"God will not, in any way, fail His beloved... Because He is never failing, we should never fear." – Hebrews 13:5

Adoration Sentence:
God, I know that I never have a reason to fear because, Your promises are never failing and You have promised me good things. You said that You have good plans for me, plans not to hurt me or leave me, but plans to give me hope and a good future. I trust in You because You are faithful to the things You say and I know You will not fail. How amazing are You, that throughout all of time You have been able to keep all of Your promises? You truly are perfect! You are perfect in every way and You never fail us.

Let's Pray Together:
I love You so much Lord, I don't know if I could tell You enough! Your ways are far beyond my ways and yet somehow You love to call me friend. You have an unfailing love and never break Your promises. You have never failed anyone! You are the perfect friend, and I get to call You mine. Thank You for always being to attentive to my needs and providing for me when I need You. I will never stop believing Your Word and trusting in You, because You are my never failing God. In Jesus name- Amen.

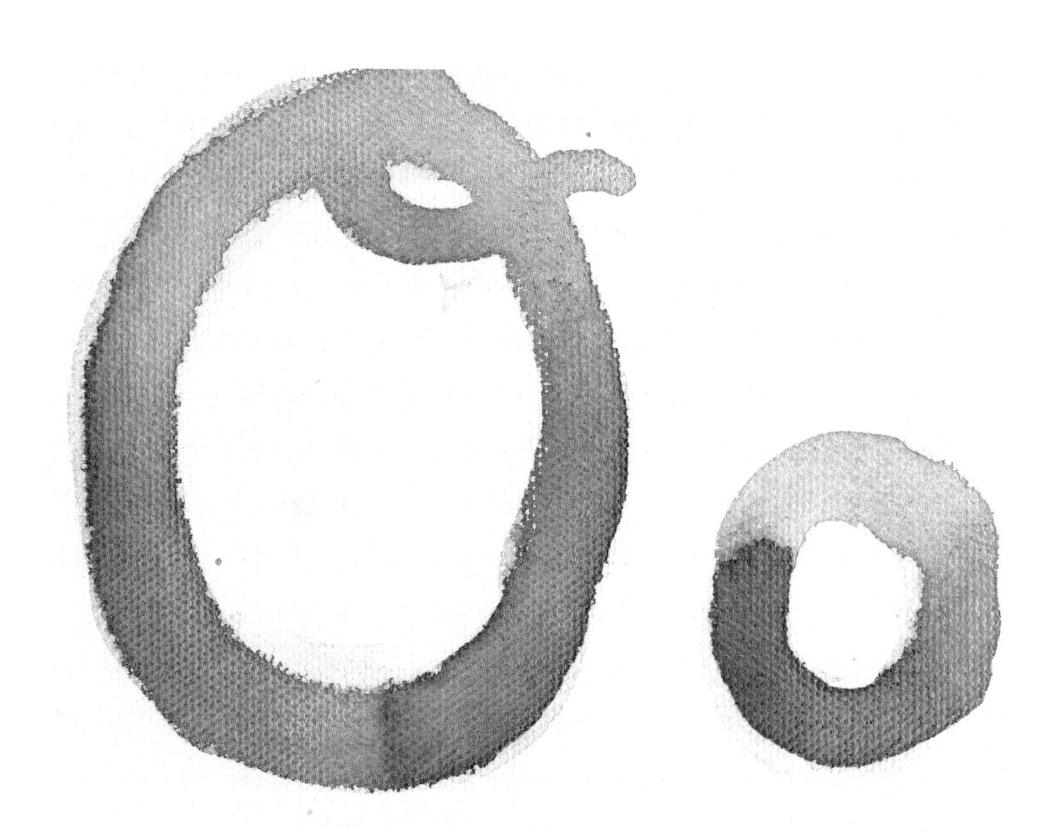
Oo

You are the **OVERCOMING GOD.**

Scripture:
"Be of good cheer! For I have overcome the world." – John 16:33

Adoration Sentence:
Jesus, everything that could be overcome; You overcame when You sacrificed Your life for us on the Cross. You overcame all sin when You rose from the grave. You have made us all over-comers, in Your name. You truly are the triumphant King who has seen His children rejoice and cheer, because You overcame the World!

Let's Pray Together:
Holy Spirit, teach me how to be a conqueror like You. I want to be as strong as my defender Jesus, who overcame the grave. Nothing is too strong for me that I cannot overcome it in Christ. Lord, show me how I can stand strong in any face of adversity and not fear. I want to walk in Your confidence because I know that You have given me Your Spirit. Thank You for raising me up like a mighty warrior and giving me the strength and confidence to overcome any situation, like You Jesus.
In Jesus name- Amen.

You are the **ONLY GOD.**

Scripture:
"And there is no other God besides me; a just God and Savior; there is none besides me." – Isaiah 45:21

Adoration Sentence:
Heavenly Father, You stand alone as the one and only God. Before time, You were the One and Only God who said, "Let there be light" and there was light! You created the Heavens and the Earth and You were the One who created humans. Your were the only One who sent a Son to save us, and then sent His Spirit to live with us. You are the Only God worthy of all praise and the Only One who will receive all of our adoration!

Let's Pray Together:
Lord, only You could breathe life into Adam and create man for the first time. Only You could come to Earth as a man, be perfect and overcome sin. Lord, only You could teach me how to love and live a righteous and holy life. Lord, You are the Only God I will ever dedicate my life to and the only One I desire to serve. Help me to show others that You are the Only way, the Truth and the Life. In Jesus name- Amen.

P p

You are the **PROVIDER GOD.**

Scripture:
"And my God shall supply all your need according to His riches in glory by Christ Jesus." – Philippians 4:19

Adoration Sentence:
Father God, I am so glad that You are our Provider. You always know how to fulfill Your children's needs. You always provide for my family and You provide for my friends. You have been the world's provision from the moment you created it. You have provided us with air to breathe, with trees to climb, with sunsets to watch and with beaches and oceans to swim! What would we do without You, our Provider. You provide us with truly everything we need and even what we might not need but desire. How good You are to us!

Let's Pray Together:
Holy Spirit, we are thankful that we can learn to receive from the Lord, through You. We have so much to receive and be thankful for because the Lord our Provider has so much to give! Thank You for providing me with a bed, and with a family and with school. Thank You for providing me with food, clothes and shelter from the rain. I am so blessed and grateful to be Your child, because I know You will never stop providing for Your beloved children! In Jesus name- Amen.

You are the **PROTECTING GOD.**

Scripture:
"'Because he loves me', says the Lord, 'I will rescue him; I will protect him and honor him, for he acknowledges My name.'" – Psalm 91:14

Adoration Sentence:
You are my covering and my defense, my sun and my shield. When I run to You I always feel safe because I know You will cover me. I desire to abide in the shadow of Your wings where I am always protected in Your love. You are my safety, no weapon can ever compare to Your Heavenly protection. You have Your angels to watch over me when I sleep at night. I will not be afraid when I have You as my Father and my protecting God!

Let's Pray Together:
Thank You God, that You love to watch over me with Your eyes of love. Thank You, that You send Your angels to protect me when I am at school or at home with my family or friends. Thank You also for watching over our nation and protecting us from harm. You can even send lots of Your angels to watch over my nation too! I believe You will protect me and my family forever. In Jesus name – Amen.

Q q

You are the **QUICK GOD.**

Scripture:
"Turn your ear to me, come quickly to my rescue, be my rock of salvation, a strong fortress to save all." – Psalm 31:2

Adoration Sentence:
Jesus, You are quick to hear my call. Lord, You are omnipresent, which means that You are everywhere. You also created time and speed, so being quick is not a problem for You! Whenever we need You or are in need of help, You are so very quick to come to our aid. We don't have to worry that You are a slow God, because You are so big and mighty that You come like a rushing wind!

Let's Pray Together:
Holy Spirit, we are so thankful that we do not have to wait long periods of time to hear from our Lord. We are able to hear from Him quickly because He is our quick God! For Him, one day is like a thousand years and a thousand years is like one day, so He can be anywhere at any time! Thank You Jesus for Your presence that is so quick to come and fill the atmosphere when we invite You in. We love and appreciate You Lord, and Your speed in answering our prayers! In Jesus name- Amen.

You are the **GOD WHO QUIETS** me with your love.

Scripture:
"The Lord your God in your midst, The Mighty One will save; He will rejoice over you with gladness, He will quiet you with his love."
– Zephaniah 3:17 (Amp)

Adoration Sentence:
Your love quiets me. It is what gets me through my day. When I think about how much You love me it satisfies my soul and makes me feel at rest. I don't have to be anxious or worried because Your perfect love throws away all of my fears. Your love is so perfect in every way it makes quiet the loud and distracting things in life. Thank You that we can be still and quiet and know that You are God!

Let's Pray Together:
My loving God, thank You for Your Peace. Your peace is so refreshing, every time I have a quiet moment and think of You I feel so at rest. I love being still and listening to Your quiet voice that whispers love into my heart. Show me how I can take time out of my day to quiet my thoughts and think only of You, so that I may adore You and shower You with my love and affection! I love You until the end of time, Lord!
In Jesus name- Amen.

Rr

You are the **REMEMBERING GOD.**

Scripture:
"He has remembered His love and His faithfulness..." – Psalm 136:23

Adoration Sentence:
I get excited when I think about the fact that You are a Remembering God. You remember all the things about me and my family, because You love us so. You remember my favorite colors, my favorite sports and games, and even my favorite things to do when I am with the ones I love. You have the best memory because You can remember everything. Even when I might forget things, You can remind me and then I can remember. I know that if I were to lose something I could ask You to help me remember where it was and I know You would be able to help me remember!

Let's Pray Together:
Jesus, You never cease to amaze me! All of Your attributes are blessings to my days. You have remembered Your children from the beginning of time, and You will never forget us. Help me to remember all of Your promises and forget not Your benefits! Thank You God for being the Lord who remembers all of our dreams, visions and our heart's desires and You never stray from fulfilling our wishes! We love You Lord and Your remembering heart! In Jesus name-Amen.

You are the **RESTORING GOD.**

Scripture:
"He restores my soul; He leads me in the paths of righteousness For His name's sake." –Psalm 23:3

Adoration Sentence:
Holy Spirit, it is You who restores my soul. You give me strength and You bring out the best in me. You are the God of restoration and You build and rebuild in my life. You have been the restoring God even since Abraham walked the Earth and You restored hope in his heart when he had his first child. No matter what comes my way, I know that I can lean on You for Your restoration power. I feel restored in you just by being in Your presence.

Let's Pray Together:
God of Restoration, this is who You truly are! Thank You for all the lives that You restore in this world. I know You have it in Your heart to restore any lost or sad people in the world. Father, could You show me how to bring restoration power and love to families, friends, different cultures, and even different countries? This is my prayer to You, that I may see Your glory shine through all my days as the God of Restoration.
In Jesus name – Amen.

Ss

You are **MY SAVIOR.**

Scripture:
"The Lord your God is in the midst of you, a Mighty One, a Savior. He will rejoice over you with joy..." – Zephaniah 3:17

Adoration Sentence:
Jesus, You are my Savior. When You gave Your life, You brought salvation into this world for the very first time. How hard it must have been for the Father to see You in pain. How much did You rejoice when You took the power from the enemy and You stood in triumph! How happy was the Father to see His children fall in love with You, Jesus? What a glorious day it was when we were able to receive salvation and begin to love You with our whole heart! And now we may spend all of eternity with You in Heaven, because we have been bought by Your love, my wonderful Savior!

Let's Pray Together:
Holy Spirit, how could we ever live without Your beautiful Presence. You have become my Savior since I was able to remember. You were my Savior when I came out of Mommy's tummy. You were my Savior on my first day of school. You were even my Savior before I asked You to live in my heart. Jesus, I would like for You to live in my heart for all the days of my life. I would also like to worship You forever for who You are, because You are my wonderful counselor and mighty Savior! In Jesus name-Amen.

You are **MY STRENGTH.**

Scripture:
"The Lord is my strength and my shield, my heart trust in Him and I am helped, my heart leaps for joy." – Psalm 28:7

Adoration Sentence:
There have been times when I did not feel so strong. I did not like those times Jesus, but with You Lord, I do feel strong. I feel very strong, because You are my strength in life. Because of You, I feel like I can do anything. The joy of the Lord, is my strength! You have shown Your strength to us, by Your actions. You gave us Your Son, and I know that took strength. Lord, in Your arms resides ALL strength.

Let's Pray Together:
Heavenly Father, Lord of all creation, thank You for being the one who provides me with strength. Throughout every day, I can lean on You for the strength I need. I feel so powerful when I say Your name Jesus. Please show me how I can be strong for others who may need strength too. I want to lift up others, the way You lift up me! I love You Jesus, and am so thankful for the strength that You have given me. In Jesus name – Amen

Tt

You are the God who **THINKS OF ME.**

Scripture:

"Many, O Lord my God are the wonderful works which You have done, and Your thoughts towards us; no one can compare with You!"
– Psalm 40:5

Adoration Sentence:

Holy Spirit, I can't believe You think of me! When I read in Your Word, that Your thoughts for me outnumber the sand on the beach, I am amazed. Why is it that You think of me? Is it because You love me? It's true! You do love me! I am ever thankful for Your love, and Your many splendored thoughts toward me. Thank You, for always having my best interest in mind, and never forgetting about me, not even for one second.

Let's Pray Together:

Father, I bless Your Holy name. Who You are, is who I want to be like. You only think good things, and You only think good thoughts of me. I pray over my life and my family's life, that we would never forget how often we are on Your mind. Holy Spirit, I want to have Your best interest at heart too, so teach me how I can love You well. I want to dwell on You for all the days of my life. In Jesus name- Amen.

You are the **TALKING GOD** who desires to talk to me.

Scripture:
"Call to me and I will answer you and tell you great and unsearchable things you do not know." – Jeremiah 33:3

Adoration Sentence:
You are the Talking God. From the beginning of time You have spoken and You created the world through Your Words. You said, "Let there be light..." and every word You spoke, came to be. You made the worlds by speaking, and You also love to speak to me. You love to speak truth to me so that I can get to know who You are and how to understand You. Jesus, You love to share Your secrets with me because You consider me Your friend!

Let's Pray Together:
God, thank You for speaking to me. Thank You, that I always have a friend in You and that You never get tired of hearing my voice or talking to me. I know that I am just learning, but can You help me to hear Your voice when You talk to me, every time? I want to hear You speak to me, like Samuel heard You speak. Can You touch my ears so that I can hear You when You whisper? Your voice is important to me, so when You speak, I will listen! In Jesus name – Amen.

You are the **UNCREATED GOD.**

Scripture:
"In the beginning was the Word and the Word was with God and the Word was God." – John 1:1

Adoration Sentence:
God, no one created You, and yet You always existed. I can't even imagine what that looks like. But even when I try to imagine a little bit, it makes me want to lift my hands, look into the sky and say, "God You are SO amazing!" You are worthy of all worship and all praise. There is no other God that compares to You. You truly are the one true GOD who is Uncreated.

Let's Pray Together:
God, I want to know You more as the Uncreated God. Through You, the Earth was made and all of the Heavens were created. You even created me. And my family, and my friends, and my school and the city I live in! God, what a wonderful creator You are. I want to worship You forever as the Uncreated God. In Jesus name – Amen.

You are the **UNDERSTANDING GOD**. Who understands me.

Scripture:
"Great is our Lord and mighty in power; His understanding has no limit."
– Psalm 147:5

Adoration Sentence:
You are my God, You are my friend and You understand me. You understand how I feel, how I think, and the desires of my heart. You understand me, because You made me and You love to get involved in my life. If the day ever comes when I feel misunderstood by others, I can always depend on Your understanding nature to comfort me. I rest in Your faithfulness towards me.

Let's Pray Together:
Father, I pray that You would help me to reach out to You, when I want to be understood. I want to look to You always, because You are my source of life and You created me. I thank You that You are tender with me and so understanding. I want to understand You too Father, so speak to my heart and help me to know You more. In Jesus name – Amen.

Vv

You are **THE VINE.**

Scripture:

"Remain in me, and I will remain in you. No branch can bear fruit by itself; it must remain in the vine. Neither can you bear fruit unless you remain in me. I am the vine; you are the branches. If a man remains in me and I in him, he will bear much fruit; apart from Me you can do nothing."
– John 15:4-5

Adoration Sentence:

You are the Vine and I am Your branch that means that life comes from You and flows through me. Apart from You (who is life) I am left to live life on my own. You never created me to live like that; You made me to be connected to You. When I am connected to You like a branch to a vine, then I start to remain in You and looking like You. Remaining in You is my safety, my peace and my hope. I want to stay connected to You forever!

Let's Pray Together:

Keep me Jesus; help me to remain in You at all times. I pray that You will keep me close to You so that I can live a life that pleases You. I know that I am not meant to live life on my own, so I ask that You help me to remember that I am a branch and I am meant to stay attached to You - the vine forever. In Jesus name – Amen.

You are **THE VICTORIOUS GOD.**

Scripture:
"But thanks be to God, who gives us the victory through our Lord Jesus Christ. - 1 Corinthians 15:57

Adoration Sentence:
Lord, You are so Victorious! Your strength is stronger than the waves in the ocean or the wind in the air. You have protected us and kept us in Your safe arms because You are truly victorious. I know that through our Lord Jesus Christ, we too can be victorious. Thank You Lord, for giving us Your strength so that we may have victory too!

Let's Pray Together:
Holy Spirit, show me what it looks like through God's eyes to truly be victorious. I want to know what it means to live victoriously and to have a victorious mindset. I want to stand for victory through all the things I do. Lord, help me to be confident and courageous like You! Thank You for being my Victorious God. In Jesus name- Amen.

Ww

You are the **WATCHFUL GOD.**

Scripture:
"The Lord will keep you from all harm; He will watch over your life.
– Psalm 121:7

Adoration Sentence:
My life is before You. You see my rising and my laying down. You know my thoughts and You see my actions. You are the God who watches me and watches over my life. You will keep me safe because Your watchful eyes are always upon me. I will not be afraid; I will put my hope in You my God. You are forever with me.

Let's Pray Together:
Lord Jesus, You are so observant. You see everything I do, and everything that goes on in my life and my family's life. You watch over us to keep us safe, and You watch over us because You care. You delight in watching Your children because they make You happy and smile. Thank You for always watching over me, my watchful God. I love You and am always thankful for You. In Jesus name- Amen.

You are **THE WISE GOD.**

Scripture:
"By wisdom the Lord laid the earth's foundations, by understanding He set the Heavens in place;" – Proverbs 3:19

Adoration Sentence:
You are such a wise God. Your wisdom is endless and available to me. The way You framed the worlds, the galaxies, even the way You made us humans; wow You are so Wise! Even the plan You had from the beginning of time to send Your son Jesus to come to the planet to die for our sins and then in His resurrection, give us access to You and all the riches of You – You are brilliant! I have no need to worry because I serve a God who is wiser than anyone I know. Bless You, my Wise God!

Let's Pray Together:
Father, You said in the book of James that if we ever lacked wisdom all we have to do is ask You, the Wise God, and You will give to us freely. So I ask for Your wisdom in to be imparted in all areas of my life. You also said in Your Word that wisdom is a very important thing to have, and that we should seek You out for wisdom. So I ask that You Holy Spirit will lead me in Your wise ways, the same way You led King Solomon, the wisest of men. In Jesus name – Amen.

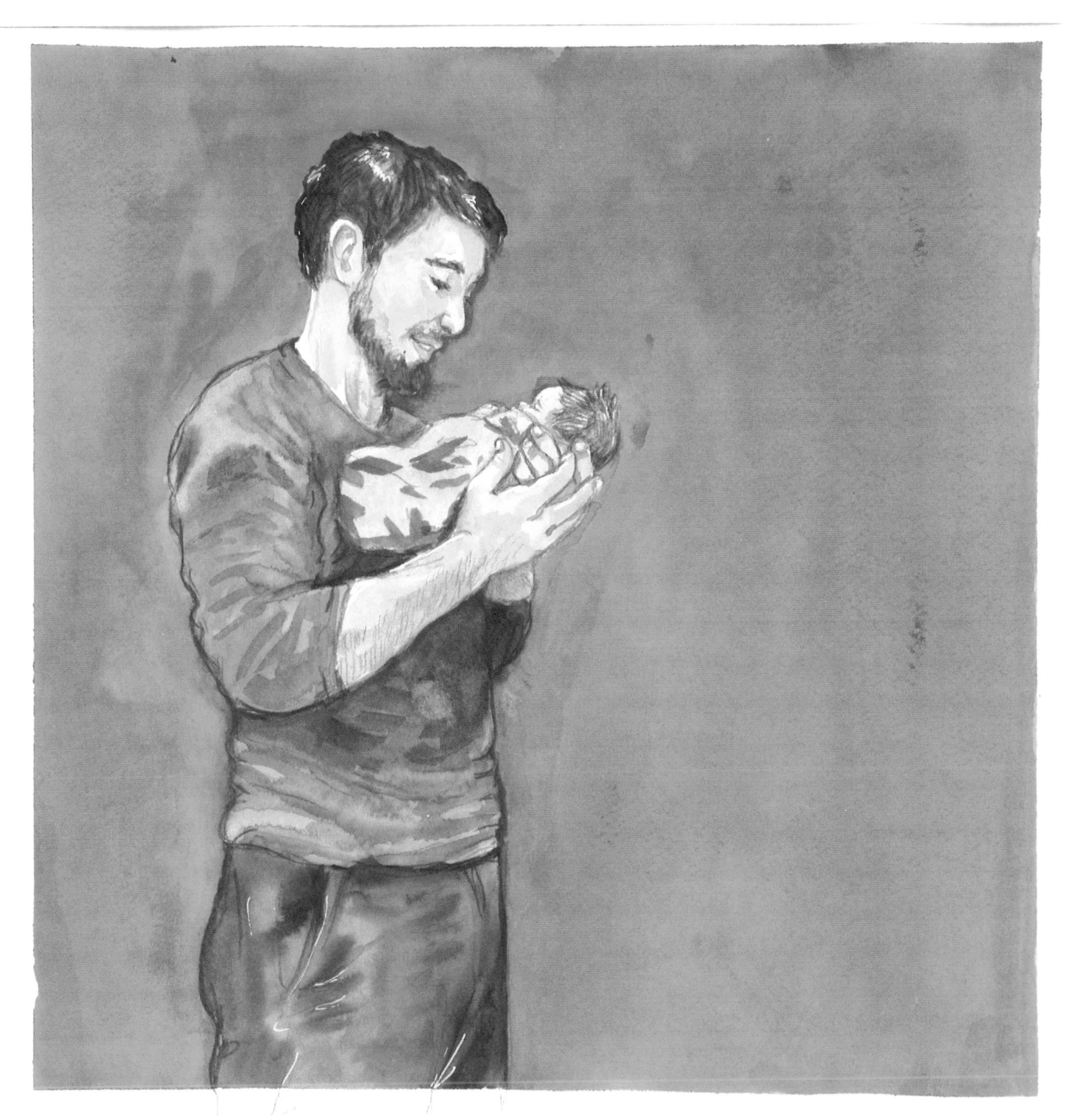

Xx

You are the **EXPERT GOD.**

Scripture:

"As for God, His way is perfect; the Word of the Lord is flawless. He is a shield for all who take refuge in Him." – Psalm 18:30

Adoration Sentence:

You are an expert in all things. There is nothing you can't do. You know about everything and everyone. If there is anything that I need help with, no matter what it is, I can always go to You for help. I am glad that I serve a God who is an expert and can lead me in the way that I should go.

Let's Pray Together:

I thank You that I can lean and depend on such a perfect God. Help me to remember that You are my expert and You have the wisdom to lead me in this life. Help me to always value Your thoughts and give me a heart to follow Your expertise always. You are my God, who knows everything! In Jesus name – Amen.

You are the **EXTRA GOD.**

Scripture:

"Now to Him who is able to do exceedingly abundantly above all that we ask or think, according to the power that works in us." – Ephesians 3:20

Adoration Sentence:

You are the overflowing, more than enough, extra God. When I think of who You are and all You possess, there is never lack, there is always extra left over for Your people. Remember when there was not enough loaves and fishes for Your people, and Jesus broke the bread and was able to feed everyone? You made extra for Your children! You are always supplying all that I need in life. I lift up my hands and receive all the extra blessings You have for me today!

Let's Pray Together:

Thank you Father that you pour blessings into my life over and over again. I know You love to give, and giving extra brings You such joy. Help me to receive Your extra grace today. Let me be aware and thankful when Your abundant love and provision are present in my life. Thank You for being such an extravagant God with my family and friends too. You are the extra God and I praise You for it. In Jesus name – Amen.

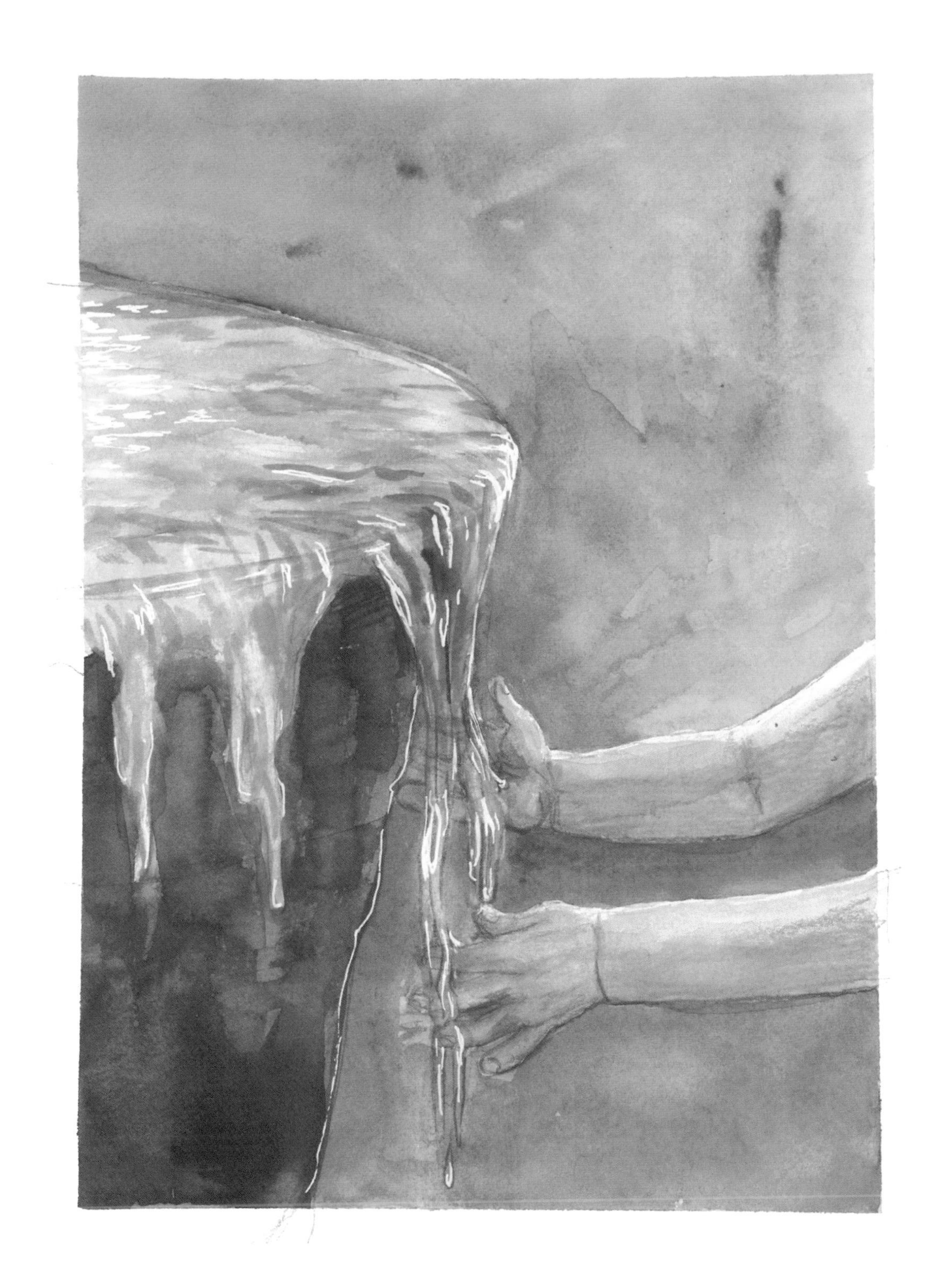

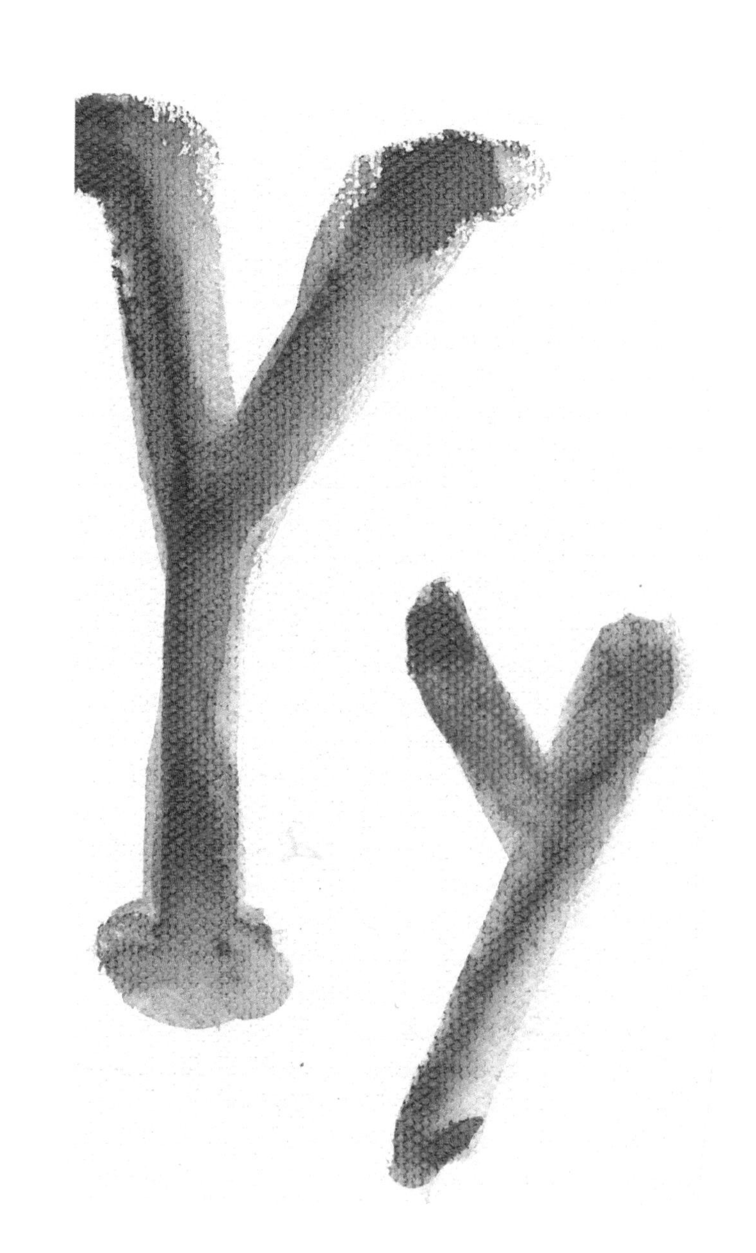

You are **YAHWEH.**

Scripture:
"Let them know You whose name is Yahweh, that You alone are the Most High over all the earth." – Psalm 83:18

Adoration Sentence:
You Jesus are Yahweh; You are the true and living God. You are the one that the prophets talked about. They all pointed to You. They told of one who would save the world and be the Messiah that Israel always longed for. I believe You are Lord, You are Yahweh!

Let's Pray Together:
Yahweh, I believe You are God, the Messiah. Lord, would You reveal to my heart the revelation of who You are? I pray that hearts all over the world would come to know You as God, and to love You as the true Messiah. The Lord of all the Heavens, You are Yahweh. In Jesus name- Amen.

You are the same **YESTERDAY**, today, and forevermore.

Scripture:
"Jesus Christ is the same yesterday, today, and forever." – Hebrews 13:8

Adoration Sentence:
God of my yesterdays, I love You. You were alive before I was born and You were there when my parents were born. You have always been, and always will be. You never change, You stay the same forever. I know that I can count on You because You are always faithful and always will be. You are the God of yesterday, today and tomorrow.

Let's Pray Together:
Thank You God, for Your unseen hand that has been calling me forth from the beginning of time. Lord, You are the King of all Kings who has no time limit. You were there for me yesterday and You will be there for me tomorrow. You are the God of now, and You never leave me. You are even preparing for me a good and hopeful future, so that I may rejoice in Your Presence forever. In Jesus name – Amen.

EMM

Zz

You are the **GOD WHO IS ZEALOUS.**

Scripture:
"The LORD shall go forth like a mighty man; He shall stir up His zeal like a man of war..." – Isaiah 42:13

Adoration Sentence:
You have strong feelings about Your promises Lord; about Your children, and about Your people of Israel. Those feelings are filled with strong passion and pursuit of the desires of Your heart. I am glad that I serve a God who feels this way about me and the promises He has made to me. May Your zeal fill up my heart with passion!

Let's Pray Together:
Zealous God, I want to feel zealous about You and about the things that are precious to Your heart. So I ask that the same zeal You have in Your heart, that You will fill me with it. I want to have a heart that wants to be with You as much as You want to be with me. I want to be known as someone who is filled with zeal for You Lord! In Jesus name – Amen.

You are the **GOD WHO IS ENTHRONED ON ZION.**

Scripture:
"From Zion, perfect in beauty, God shines forth." – Psalm 50:2

Adoration Sentence:
Jesus, my King on Mt. Zion, You are Lord. Zion is your mountain, it is Your beautiful city. Your Word in Psalm 48 says there will be rejoicing and gladness on Mount Zion, because it is Your city, and it is where You reign forever and ever. I will praise You all my days, my glorious King who reigns on Mount Zion!

Let's Pray Together:
Jesus, I want to see what a beautiful city Mount Zion is. Lord, would You show me where it is that You reign. I want to dwell in the house of the Lord forever. I want to sit on Mt. Zion with You Lord, and look out across the Earth at Your creation. You above all Lord, are worthy of all praise and I want to adore You for all eternity! In Jesus name- Amen.

Other Resources Available By Deeper Waters:

Bobhartley.org

For More Illustrations by E. M. M. Clonts:

www.facebook.com/pages/EMM-Illustrate/178142495537491
emm.illustrate@gmail.com

CPSIA information can be obtained
at www.ICGtesting.com
Printed in the USA
LVIW010835031212
309780LV00002B